PRESENTED TO

CHRISTIE BAILEY

FROM

Miss H.

12-9-01

To remember your Baptism

Water, Come Down!

To the tender Cassindra Marie
my granddaughter
at the start of her life under God

WATER, COME DOWN!
The Day You Were Baptized

Text copyright © 1999 Walter Wangerin, Jr.
Illustrations copyright © 1999 Augsburg Fortress

Published in association with the literary agency of Alive Communications, P.O. Box 49068, Colorado Springs, CO 80949.

Cover design by Marti Naughton
Book design by Michelle L. Norstad

Library of Congress Cataloging-in-Publication Data
Wangerin, Walter.
   Water, Come Down! : the day you were baptized / Walter Wangerin, Jr.
     p. cm.
   Includes bibliographical references.
   Summary: Sun, cloud, rain, wind, water, and the whole of creation
join family and friends in celebrating the baptism of a child of God.
   ISBN 0-8066-3711-0 (alk. paper)
   1. Baptism—Juvenile literature [1. Baptism.] I. Title.
   BV811.2.W36 1999
   265′.1—dc21   99-25819
                                          CIP

The paper used in this publication meets the minimum requirements of American National Standard for Information Sciences—Permanence of Paper for Printed Library Materials, ANSI Z329.48-1984. ⊖ ™

Manufactured in Hong Kong. Printed by C & C Offset Printing Co., Ltd.   AF 9-3711

04   03   02   01   4   5   6   7   8   9   10

Water, Come Down!

The Day You Were Baptized

Walter Wangerin, Jr.

Augsburg

MINNEAPOLIS

I am the sun.
I am fire and light.
I'm the first one
At the end of the night
Who heard of your naming day.

God told me to whisper
The news to my sister:
A child will be named today.

I am the cloud, high, white, and proud,
Or black and flashing, roaring out loud:
  I never could
  Hide my mood.

So on the day when the sun came by
To whisper that *you* were to be baptized,
   To be washed in the fire of God,
   And to shine with the light of God,
I laughed. O child, I laughed till I cried,
Till the tears of rejoicing ran down from my eyes;
   Thunder I thundered out loud
   For the kid who is loved by a cloud.

I am the rain coming down from heaven,
One drop,
Ten drops,
Ten million and seven,
Down, down, to water the ground
To make the good grain grow.

But on the day when *you* were baptized
I rode the wind to the edge of the skies
And cried to the sun, "Sun, shine on me
For the child below, so the child can see
    A flaming raining-bow!"

So after the rainstorms, dear child of mine,
Whenever you see it, that rainbow's a sign
That God is with you; and God is kind:
 He'll never let you go.

I am the wind. I blow the rain
Like needles against your windowpane,
Or I carry it down in misty showers
To rinse the trees and wash the flowers.
No one can see me, but I am the power,
    The breath and the spirit of God.

That day when the sun told the cloud about you,
And the cloud told the rain, and the rain told me, too,
    I wanted to wash you, clean and good;
I wanted to blow that water to you
    Fast, as fast as I could.

But the earth below was cracked and drying;
Trees, no leaves. The flowers, dying—
    And seeds could do no good.

So I poured the rain on the thirsty ground
Which drank—and drank the good seed down,
    The seed that makes your food.

I am the seed that grows the wheat
That makes the bread the children eat;
   but I, before I rise,
Before I grow, I go deep down:
I die, the dark earth underground.
Water gives me life again,
   And I become the golden grain.

I am the water that came from God,
From the love of the sun and his sister, the cloud,
  The water that filled the skies.

And I am the water of colors, for we
(The rain and the sun and the wind and me)
  Made a bow at the edge of the skies.

And I am the water went under the ground
To turn the whole world upside down,
    To bring the dead to life.

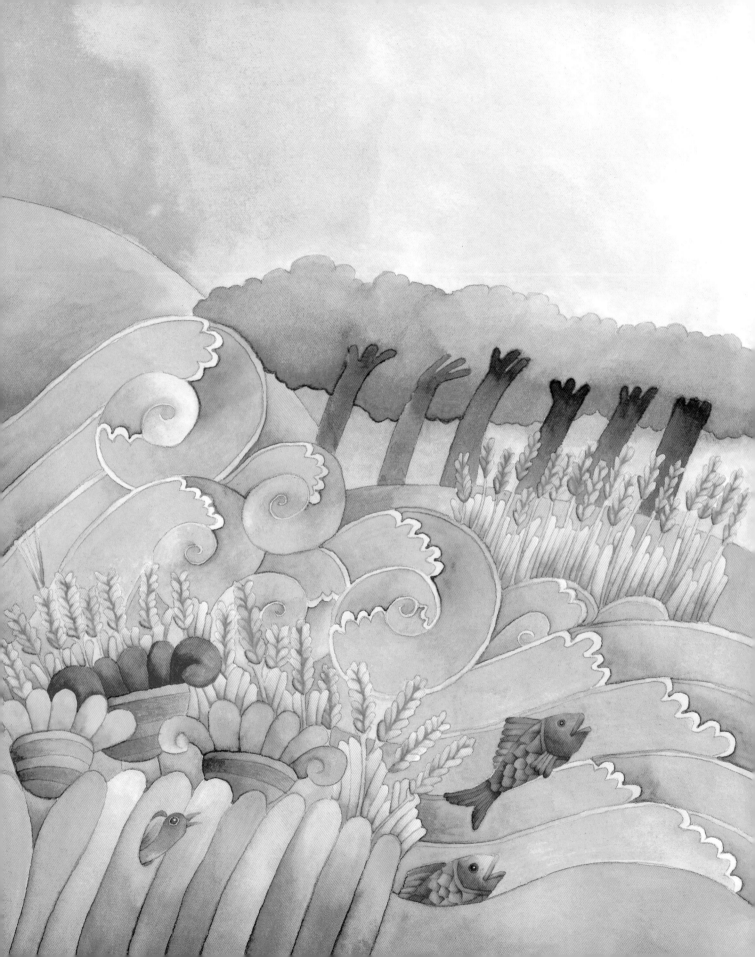

And I am the water that flows in a river,
The River of Life, forever and ever—
Yes! I am the water came down to your town,
To find *you*, child, and you I found—
    The day you were baptized.

I am the water they washed you in,
Your head, your heart, your soul, your skin,
Clean of the devil! Clean from sin,
   The day you were baptized.

Your family was there that holy day,
They heard the good Baptizer say,
In the name of the Father and of the Son
And of the Spirit, Three in One,
   I baptize you, dear child.

I am the water that fell on you
Three times with the Word that made you new
While everyone smiled and smiled.

Upon your forehead, the cross of Christ;
And in your hand, the light of his light!
   O child of earth and skies:
Burning as bright as the angels at night,
You are God's love and God's loveliest sight
   On the day you were baptized.

All of us, now, on earth and in heaven,
One mouth,
Ten mouths,
Ten million and seven,
Greet you, friend. We're glad you came—
So glad we stand and applaud.

And we call you by your brand-new name;
Beautiful, beautiful child of flame,
You are the *Child of God*.

The Story of Baptism

God created everything: light and sky and water, sun and moon and stars, vegetable life and animal life—and us. Human beings.

It would have been fine. All would have been well between us and God and everything else; but sin entered in. Our sin separated us from God. It even grieved creation, as St. Paul says in Romans 8: "The creation waits with eager longing for the revealing of the children of God . . . in hope that the creation itself will be set free from its bondage to decay."

As in sin, so in grace: all creation is bound together. When God reaches down to love us and to adopt us by Baptism, creation itself rejoices in the "revealing of the children of God."

So I've written a story in which both God and creation delight in a particular child—in *your* child. And I've drawn upon the rich heritage of Scripture throughout. Each speaker of God's glad word (sun, cloud, rain, wind) also carries a sacred meaning. And the best person to reveal that meaning to your child is you.

On the following pages I have identified the Bible passages you may use to tell your child the "rest of the story." Read the biblical texts by yourself first, then share them with the child in your own words. Talk about their meaning for both of you, children of God through Baptism. Talk about your own experience with these two Baptisms—yours and the child's.

And here are ways to enhance the settings for your discussions.

• Bring out memorabilia of the child's Baptism: a baptismal gown, certificate, photographs.

• Light a candle—a baptismal candle, if you have one.

• Go outside to see and feel the sun, the wind, the rain—or to view a rainbow.

• Plant a seed and let the child tend and water it. Together watch it come to new life from its "grave" in the soil.

• Visit your church after services to study the symbols and baptismal font.

• And surely, attend Baptisms at church with your child.

God bless you and your child in this wonderful teaching!

Walt Wangerin

Walter Wangerin, Jr., Valparaiso, Indiana

"I am the sun. I am fire and light."

The sun—a glorious image of God's creating light and a reminder of Jesus, the Son of Righteousness.

Genesis 1:1-4. Let the sun in *Water, Come Down!* be the Light of God, created at the beginning of the world.

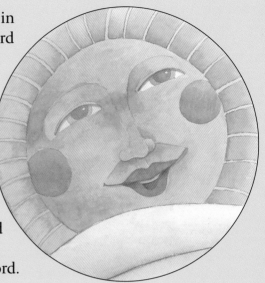

John 1:1-5. Make a direct connection to the opening verses in John's Gospel: "In the beginning was the Word, and the Word was with God, and the Word was God. . . . What has come into being in him was life, and the life was the light of all people. The light shines in the darkness, and the darkness did not overcome it." That light, that Sun of Righteousness, is Jesus come among us now! This is the light now knowing and shining on the child.

Isaiah 9:2, 6. Read together the verses in Isaiah to embellish what the light does. Again, make the connection to Jesus in the birth described in verse 6: "Unto us [you] a child is born." Parallel that Holy Child and your child—who was made a child of God in Baptism, a sister or brother of the Lord.

"I am the cloud, high, white, and proud."

The Shekinah, the "presence" of God made evident in the lives of God's people, has often been pictured as a cloud.

Exodus 13:21-22; 14:19-25. Mercifully, it was the cloud of God's presence that protected Israel from armies of Egypt at the Red Sea, and then led them through the sea and wilderness to the Promised Land. Through the waters of Baptism, the child is led to the eternal Promised Land—life with God that never ends.

Exodus 19:16—20:17. It was a cloud on Mount Sinai that represented the law-giving God who delivered to the people the Ten Commandments—lovingly teaching them how to live the new life with God.

Matthew 17:1-8. On the Mount of Transfiguration, the Cloud and the Voice together named Jesus as Son of God—and, through Jesus, they name the child as one of God's own.

"I am the rain coming down from heaven."

Rain—a symbol of cleansing, of life, of God's life-giving Word.

Isaiah 55:10, 11. Read God's words through the prophet Isaiah. In Baptism, it is water and the Word of God—both miraculous sources of life—that bring new life to the child.

Genesis 6:11—9:17. Read together the account of the Flood—in the Bible first, then (if you wish) in a popularized retelling of the story. Notice how rain accomplishes two purposes: it washes the earth clean of evil; and it also saves people.

1 Peter 3:20b-22. Peter describes how eight persons were saved in the waters of the Flood, and how this water signifies Baptism, in which water and the Word of God together wash the child—not of dirt, but as an appeal to God for a good conscience, through the resurrection of Jesus Christ. This is a good chance to show that, as with the Flood, someone died and someone lived. Jesus died so that the child can live.

"Whenever you see it, that rainbow's a sign."

The rainbow is a reminder of God's faithful promise, connected with water.

Genesis 9:8-17. Read the conclusion to the Flood story, in which God makes a promise to Noah and to the whole wide world. This is a promise the child can trust—that you can trust. Talk about the rainbow in the sky after rain: a reminder, always, of God's promise. Talk about the promise God makes in Baptism.

"I am the wind. I blow the rain."

Wind is a picture of God's powerful, life-giving Spirit.

Genesis 1:1-3; 2:7. Return to the Creation story. God's spirit ("a wind from God") was present at the beginning. Note, in Genesis 2, how God "formed man from the dust of the ground, and breathed into his nostrils the breath of life, and man became a living being." Wind and Spirit create life.

The Spirit ("a wind from God") was there at Creation with the Voice ("And God said...") and the Light ("Let there be light"). Talk about how these three represent the Trinity—the wholeness of God: Father-Creator-Voice; Son-Light-Child; Spirit-Wind-Breath of God. And parallel the clay-person's coming to life with the child's coming to life through Baptism, also from God.

John 20:19-23. When he appeared to his disciples, the risen Jesus blew upon them, saying, "Receive the Holy Spirit." That's the wind that loves the child.

". . . thirsty ground which drank . . . the good seed down"

The ground and the seed are images for the child, who needs God's life-giving water to blossom and grow.

Isaiah 55:10, 11. Again remind the child how rain makes the earth bloom with life.

John 12:24. Jesus prepares his disciples for his death and resurrection by telling them how a seed needs to die in order to live again. Talk about two deaths and two resurrections: Jesus died and was buried, but he came to life again—like the dead earth that lives anew each spring.

Romans 6:3, 4. Explain St. Paul's words: the child, too, died to all bad things, cuddled down like a seed deep in the earth, but came up new and fresh and green in Jesus. In Baptism, sin dies; but the life that rises from Baptism lasts forever.

"All of us, now, on earth and in heaven"

Talk about the church building—the one pictured in the story and the building in which your child was baptized—and the signs and symbols it offers. Then expand an understanding of "church." This is the place where the Baptisms happen—the spiritual place as much as the physical one.

This is the place where baptized people gather; and in their gathering, the place becomes the Church of Jesus, that is . . .

• those who are close to the child are his or her family (and let the parents who read the story also speak of their faith in, and love for, Jesus);

• all Christians everywhere in the world are now the family of this child;

• and all believers who ever lived—and all who will live—rejoice with this Baptism, welcome the child both into this worldly existence and, at the same time, into the eternal family where many mothers and fathers and saints and martyrs and angels exist already, awaiting the child's final arrival. Adam and Eve are there, the Children of Israel are there, Noah is there, Isaiah is there, the apostles John, Peter, and Paul are there. Jesus is there. All rejoicing.